MW01104747

DEFINITELY FROM OUT OF TOWN

by Seth Jarvis

Illustrated by Nathan Y. Jarvis

Published by Capstone Press, Inc.

Distributed By

℗ CHILDRENS PRESS ®

CHICAGO

CIP
LIBRARY OF CONGRESS CATALOGING IN PUBLICATION DATA

Jarvis, Seth.
Definitely from out of town / by Seth Jarvis.
p. cm.-- (Star shows)
Summary: Cathy and Danny like to watch people and speculate about their backgrounds but they are surprised when a short kid with unusual clothes walks up to them and tells them he is "definitely from out of town," in fact, from another planet.

ISBN 1-56065-008-7

1. Life on other planets--Juvenile literature. [1. Planets. 2. Outer space. 3. Astronomy.] I. Title. II. Series.
QB54.J33 1989
574.999--dc20   90-1353 CIP AC

Designed by Nathan Y. Jarvis & Associates, Inc.

Capstone Press

Box 669, Mankato, MN, U.S.A. 56001

CONTENTS

PEOPLE WATCHING

CATHY AND DANNY sat on a bench at the zoo. Their mom had let them spend the whole day there. They were taking a rest before starting for home. They watched people walking by. There were big people and little, skinny and fat, some with big noses and some with small mouths. They began playing a game they had made up. They called it "people-watching."

The rules were easy. One of them would be the "spotter." The spotter would find a person in the crowd. Then the spotter would take a piece of paper and write a clue about that person. The "guesser" had to read the clue and write down who he thought the person was. Cathy and Danny didn't stare at the people they were watching. That gave away the answer. Besides, they knew it was rude to stare.

It was fun to think of short, clever ways to describe the people they saw.

Cathy got to be the spotter. She looked at the people around them. Then she wrote, "Oh give me a home where the buffalo roam," and passed the clue to Danny. He looked around. Soon he picked out a man dressed in cowboy boots, blue jeans, and a cowboy hat.

"Cowboy boots and hat. Easy." Danny wrote on the paper and handed it back to Cathy. She looked around again. She saw two people and wrote one word, "Vacation." She handed the paper back to Danny. He looked around and saw a man and woman. Both were wearing shorts, sandals, T-shirts, baseball caps, and sunglasses. Both had cameras on straps around their necks. Danny wrote on the paper "Cameras, caps, shades — tourists. My turn to be spotter."

THE STRANGE KID

Danny was just about to start writing a clue for a woman in coveralls. Then he noticed a very short kid in a floppy hat and strange clothes that were way too big. He was walking very slowly toward them. Danny wrote on the paper, "From out of town." He handed it back to Cathy. She read it and was about to complain that it wasn't a fair clue. Then she saw the short kid. The kid walked up and sat down on the bench right in between Danny and her!

The short kid didn't move. Cathy and Danny didn't move. Nobody said a word. Cathy and Danny were feeling very uncomfortable.

A few seconds passed. Then the kid sighed loudly and said, "Whew! Made it! What a relief! But you know, I'm kind of disappointed. You all look so much alike."

Cathy and Danny looked at the short kid. They looked at each other. They couldn't see the kid's face because it was covered by a floppy hat, sunglasses, and the collar of a much-too-big overcoat.

"Excuse me?" Danny said to the kid.

"I said I'm glad to be here, but I'm kind of disappointed. You all look so much alike," the kid repeated.

"Who looks alike?" asked Cathy.

"You!" said the kid. "You're all the same. Two eyes, two ears, two arms, two legs, 10 fingers, 10 toes. You're all the same."

Danny stared at the short kid. He thought about what the short kid had said.

"We are not all the same," he answered. "Some people are big and some people are small. Some people have dark skin and some people have light skin. Cathy's got blond hair. I've got brown hair. Cathy's left-handed and I'm right-handed. Our mom's got blue eyes, and our dad's got brown eyes."

The short kid was quiet for a moment and then spoke. "How many bones do you have in your neck? I'll tell you. Seven. You have seven, she has seven, you all have seven." The short kid pointed behind them at a giraffe. "Even a giraffe on this planet has seven bones

in its neck. And it has two eyes, one nose, two nostrils, two lungs, two kidneys."

Cathy and Danny stared at each other. They were wondering if they'd each heard the same thing. "Even a giraffe on this planet..."

"Are you from around here?" Cathy asked.

The short kid answered her. "No, I'm from... well... You might say I'm from out of town."

"I knew it!" said Danny.

Cathy looked hard at the short kid. "You're from farther away than that. You're not even from Earth, are you."

The short kid wiggled a little, then finally said, "Well, so? What if I'm not?"

"Ha!" said Danny. "Definitely from out of town!"

"What's your name?" Cathy asked.

The short kid thought for a moment, then answered, "You can call me Doot."

"Doot? What kind of a name is that?" asked Cathy.

"I just made it up," said Doot. "D-O-O-T. It means Definitely Out Of Town."

"But what's your real name?" Danny asked.

"Oh, I can't tell you that," Doot said.

"Where I come from, you don't tell someone your real name until you know them very well. In fact, it's considered quite rude to tell someone your name as soon as you meet them."

"That's crazy!" Cathy said. "Who are you really? And what are you doing here?"

"I'm doing my homework," Doot said. "I'm supposed to write a report on how different kinds of life on different planets look different from each other. This is the fifty-fourth planet I've visited. I decided to land in a zoo because I thought that way I'd see a lot of different kinds of Earth creatures at once. As far as I can see though, living things here look pretty much alike. This planet has average gravity, average air, average temperature, and average light. It seems pretty bland to me."

"How can you say that things are all the same?" Danny said. "Didn't you see how different all the animals in the zoo are? We've got animals here that are really big. Didn't you see the elephants? And there are even bigger animals in the oceans — whales! They're really big! And some things on Earth are really tiny, like bugs. There are bugs so small you have to use a microscope just to see them!"

"And what about plants?" Cathy asked. "Plants breathe in carbon dioxide and then

11

breathe out oxygen. Animals are just the opposite. They breathe in oxygen and breathe out carbon dioxide. You can't say we're that much alike."

Doot thought about it for a moment and then said, "OK, maybe there are a few differences. But they're not like the differences between here and some of the other places I've been. I know about a place where there are flying animals the size of mountains! You can't tell me you've got anything like that here."

"Well of course not," said Danny. He thought about an animal the size of a mountain and tried to imagine it flying. But that didn't make much sense to him. "How can an animal that big fly?" he asked.

"Well it couldn't fly here," said Doot. "This planet's air is too thin. The planet I'm thinking of is much bigger."

Doot made a funny squeaking noise. Suddenly a picture of Earth appeared. Next to it was a picture of a planet several times bigger than Earth. "A big planet like this weighs more than Earth. That means the bigger planet has more **gravity** than Earth. The extra gravity holds on to more air, so the air is a lot thicker. Animals can swim through the thick air just like fish swim in water here on Earth."

Suddenly a picture of a gigantic creature floated in front of them. The creature looked kind of like a huge lumpy balloon. It hovered above a strange looking city in a shimmering, reddish-pink sky. "This is called a Blimp Beast," Doot said.

BLIMP BEASTS AND
TUMBLE CRITTERS

Cathy and Danny's eyes were wide with amazement as they watched the pictures floating in front of them.

"How do you do that?" Cathy asked.

"Oh that?" Doot said. "It's nothing. You draw pictures on paper, I draw pictures in the air. It's no big deal."

Cathy and Danny both wondered what would be a big deal to Doot. Before they could ask, Doot had made a new picture in front of them.

"If you want to see something really weird, you ought to go to this planet. The winds there blow like crazy all the time. This is where the Tumble Critters live. Tumble Critters are small and don't weigh much. They have hundreds of legs all around them that stick out in all directions. At the end of each leg is a small claw. They hang on to the ground with

their claws to keep from blowing away in the strong wind.

"Tumble Critters can't move very well on their own. When they want to go somewhere, they wait for the wind to blow in the direction they want. Then they let go of whatever they're hanging on to. They roll along the ground with the wind. When they want to stop or change directions, they grab on to the ground with their claws.

"Tumble Critters aren't very smart. Sometimes hundreds and hundreds of them all get blown together in a big ball. It takes days for them to figure out how to slow down and get untangled.

Cathy was watching the picture of Tumble Critters in amazement. "What do they eat?" she asked.

"Tumble Critters eat grass," Doot said. "They use their little claws to grab small bunches of grass as they roll along the ground."

"Are there Blimp Beasts on that planet?" Danny asked.

Doot looked surprised by the question. "Oh no! The planet's not at all the right kind for Blimp Beasts."

Danny didn't understand what Doot meant by that. "Why not?" he asked.

"Look around you!" Doot said, waving an arm toward the animals in the zoo. "All of the animals here are just the right kind for Earth. And Earth is just the right kind of planet for all of them. Don't you see?"

Doot could tell by the puzzled looks on their faces that they didn't. "All right," began Doot. "Look at that polar bear. Look at it carefully. Pretend you haven't any idea where polar bears usually live. Does the way the polar bear looks tell you anything about where it lives?"

Cathy stared at the big bear. She said, "Well, it's got a thick coat of fur, so you know it probably came from somewhere that's pretty cold."

"And the white color of the fur looks like it could blend in with white snow so the bear would be hard to see when it hunts for food," Danny added.

"And the bear's big padded feet are kind of like snow shoes. Those would help it walk across soft snow without falling through," Cathy said.

"All those things show that the bear is probably from a place that is cold and snowy," Danny said.

"Perfect!" said Doot. "That's the idea. Polar bears look the way they do because of where they live. They're made for cold and snowy places. Now then, what about those animals over there?"

Cathy and Danny looked. Doot was pointing to the hippopotamus pen. One big hippo was standing near the edge of a pool. Another hippo was in the pool, almost completely covered with water.

Doot asked Cathy and Danny, "From the way those animals look, where do you think they spend most of their time. On the land or in the water?"

Danny looked at the hippos for a moment. "They look really big and fat," he said. "I'll bet they'd have a hard time moving around on the ground with all that weight. I'll say they spend most of their time in the water. In the water they wouldn't have all that weight on their feet."

"I think he's right, but for a different reason," said Cathy. "Look at how the hippo's eyes and nose are all the way up on top of its head. It has its nose just above the water so it can breathe. And its eyes are just above the water so it can see. That lets most of the hippo be under water."

"Do polar bears and hippos live in the same places?" asked Doot.

"No way!" said Danny.

"But if you'd never seen them before, how could you know that?" Doot asked.

Cathy and Danny stared at the hippos. Neither one of them could think of an answer. Doot asked another question. "When is it best to sit in a lake, when it's cold outside or when it's hot?"

"When it's hot of course," Danny said. "You jump in the lake to cool off. Nobody sits in a lake to get warm."

"I've got it!" said Cathy. "If hippos sit in the water to stay cool, then that must mean it gets hot where they live. Hippos come from hot places. Polar bears don't."

"Now you're getting the idea," said Doot. "You can sometimes tell a lot about where things come from by studying what they look like."

"I get it. Hey, you know what this is like?" Danny said to Cathy. "This is just like our people-watching game. Only instead of people, you look at animals."

Danny thought for a moment. Then he said, "Hey! You can play the game backward, too! We always look at someone and try to

20

figure out where they're from. Now we can look at a faraway place and imagine what someone from there might look like!"

"How far away are you talking about?" Doot asked.

"Oh, I don't know," Danny said. "China or Argentina, places like that."

"You call that far away?" Doot asked. "Tell me, how many noses do the people there have? How many lungs, or toes, or eyes or stomachs? How many arms and legs? People on Earth are people. Like I said before, you're all the same. If you want to make your game fun, you have to imagine places farther away than somewhere on this planet. You've got to think about places that are really far away."

IMAGINING LIFE ON THE MOON

"Okay then," Cathy said. "I'm going to think about what people might look like if their home was the moon."

"Do you really think that will work?" Doot asked. "I'm not sure if you understand about your moon. First of all, your moon hasn't..."

Danny interrupted. "Moon creatures! Yeah! They'd be great big monsters with yellow and red bug-eyes and green slimy skin and they'd have thirteen heads and..."

"Wait!" cried Doot. "You're not thinking about it. Take it one step at a time. Start at the beginning. What do you know about your moon?"

"It's covered with **craters** and it's smaller than Earth," said Cathy.

"And it goes around Earth in an orbit," said Danny.

"Now you're getting somewhere," Doot said. "Now you've got a good place to start."

With that, Doot made a squeaking noise. Again there appeared a picture floating in front of the three of them. This time the picture was of the Earth and moon floating next to each other in space. Earth was a large, pretty blue ball. The moon was a much smaller, round gray ball covered with craters of all sizes.

"Why are the Earth and moon so different from each other?" Doot asked. "They both go around the sun at the same distance. That means they get the same amount of light and heat. They're both about the same age. And they're pretty much made out of the same kinds of rocks. How come the moon is covered with craters and Earth isn't?"

"Because the moon hasn't got an **atmosphere**, but Earth does," Cathy said.

"The atmosphere burns up **meteors** before they can hit the ground," Danny added.

"I think you've got the answer half right and half wrong," Doot said. "Have you ever seen a shooting star?" Cathy and Danny nodded yes.

"Meteors are the same things as **shooting stars**," said Cathy. "They're pieces of rock from outer space burning up in the air."

"Most of the meteors you see at night are made by pieces of rock no bigger than a pebble," Doot said. "They enter your atmosphere at a very fast speed. The friction of the air rubbing against them makes them so hot that they burn up. But what about pieces of rock that are bigger than a pebble? What if the rock that entered your atmosphere was the size of a car? Would it burn up?"

Cathy and Danny thought about it for a minute. "I don't think so," said Danny. "I think that it might be too big."

"You're right," Doot said. "It would be burned a little, but it would still hit the ground. Now then, what about a rock the size of a house that weighed thousands and thousands of tons? What do you suppose would happen if it went zooming through the Earth's atmosphere toward the ground?"

"BOOM!" shouted Cathy. "It would smash into the Earth!"

"And leave a big crater!" shouted Danny.

"Very good!" said Doot. "Now think about this. The moon is covered with craters that were made by rocks the size of mountains hitting it. The Earth has been hit by at least as many rocks as the moon has, probably more, why doesn't Earth's surface have craters like the moon?"

"Oh, I know!" said Danny. "The craters on Earth got erased by the rain and wind. It's called **erosion**. The rain and wind wore down the craters so much that they disappeared."

Doot pointed to the picture of the moon in front of them. "The moon has no air. Its gravity is too weak to hold onto an atmosphere. Without an atmosphere, there's no water or wind to cause erosion. That's why the moon is covered with craters — no erosion.

"There's another difference between Earth and the moon. On Earth the air works like a blanket. It evens out the temperatures between the shadows and sunlight. On the moon, though, the temperature in the sunlight gets as high as 260° Fahrenheit. But the temperature in the shade is around 250° below zero! Brrr!

"So you tell me. What kind of life might you find on a place where there is no air or water and where the temperature changes by more than 500° between sunlight and shadow?"

Cathy and Danny looked at the picture of the Earth and moon in front of them. Then Danny turned to Doot. "I guess there probably isn't any life on the moon. It would just be too hard for something to live there."

"You've got it!" said Doot. "Sometimes you have to admit that a place is just too nasty for life to exist."

26

IMAGINING LIFE ON VENUS

"What about another planet? Venus is the same size as Earth isn't it?" Cathy asked. "Maybe we could imagine what life might be like on a planet like Venus."

"Venus? Owww!" cried Doot. "I don't even like to think about that place. Don't you know about Venus?" Doot made a squeaking sound and a picture of Venus and Earth popped into view. "Sure, it's about the same size as Earth, but it's still the nastiest of nasty places to look for life. Day or night, north pole, equator or south pole, the temperature on Venus is always around 900° Fahrenheit. That's more than twice as hot as the inside of an oven! It's so hot on Venus that at night the rocks on the ground glow red-hot. What kind of life could exist on a planet like that?"

"OK," said Cathy. "I see what you mean. Maybe Venus isn't such a good place to imagine

life. But what about Mars? Couldn't there be life on Mars? I read in school that Mars has an atmosphere and that it used to have rivers full of water."

"Yes I suppose so. But Mars would still be a pretty rough place to live," said Doot. A picture of Earth and Mars appeared in front of them. "You're right about Mars having an atmosphere. But you've got to remember that there's not very much of it. Martian air would have to be a hundred times thicker than it is now before it was as thick as the air on Earth. And whatever water Mars once had is mostly gone now. There probably is some water frozen in the ground or in the Martian ice caps, but otherwise Mars is a big frozen rock. If there is life on Mars, it might be something simple, like a kind of moss that grows on the sides of rocks."

Just then a voice came booming over a loudspeaker. "Attention visitors, the zoo will be closing in ten minutes!"

"Oops!" Doot said. "It's getting late. I need to get going."

"But you haven't told us about a place where aliens live!" Cathy said.

"I've got an idea," Danny said. "You can come home and have dinner with us. Have you ever ridden on a bus?"

"I don't think so," Doot said. "I think I would remember if I had. What's a bus?"

"Are you kidding?" Cathy asked. "A bus carries people from one place to another. But we've got to hurry if we're going to catch the one that will take us home. You can tell us about planets with aliens on them on the way. Come on, let's run!"

"Not so fast!" cried Doot. "The gravity on your planet is awful. I'm still too tired to walk again. I'm sure there's no way I could run."

"What do you mean you're tired?" Cathy asked. "All you've been doing is sitting on this bench. How can you be tired? And besides, what's wrong with the gravity here?"

"You're used to this gravity," said Doot. "It's the only gravity you've ever known. The planet where I come from is a little smaller. Its gravity isn't as powerful as the gravity is here. I'm still getting used to it. It takes just about all of my energy to sit upright. I like the idea of riding something right now, I really do. But not if I have to run. Maybe you'd better go on without me."

"I know," Danny said. "We'll carry you!"

In a flash Danny picked up Doot. "You hardly weigh anything!" Danny said. "I can carry you by myself, no sweat." A moment later Doot was sitting on Danny's shoulders as Cathy and Danny ran to the bus stop.

Doot bounced up and down on Danny's shoulders as they ran. He wondered what kind of strange animal this "bus" was that they were running to capture.

The three of them arrived at the bus stop a few minutes later. Cathy and Danny were tired from running and sat down on a bench. Danny let Doot stay on his shoulders.

"Why are we stopping here?" Doot asked. "I thought we were running to catch a bus."

"We were," Cathy said. "This is where we catch it."

"It must not be a very smart bus if it can see you waiting here to catch it and it still comes right to you," Doot said.

"No, you don't understand," Danny said. "A bus is a machine. You ride inside it to get from one place to another. Look! Here it comes! We got here just in time."

A big city bus rolled to a stop in front of them. The doors whooshed open. Cathy and Danny stood up to climb inside. But Doot seemed to be afraid of it.

"What's wrong?" Cathy asked. "It's just a bus. Come on and get in or it'll leave without us."

Doot whispered in a frightened voice, "It looks just like a Side Biter! Are you sure it's not going to eat us?"

The bus driver called down to them. "Are you kids getting on or not?"

"It's only a bus," Cathy said as she and Danny climbed inside. Doot was still on Danny's shoulders.

Cathy and Danny sat down in the very back of the bus. Danny put Doot down between them again.

SIDE BITERS, HOOP WORMS, AND PUFF BUGS

As soon as the three of them were settled in their seats, Cathy asked Doot, "What's a Side Biter?"

"Oh, you'll want to stay clear of them!" Doot warned. "They're about as big as this bus and kind of shaped like it. They have short, thick legs, and their mouths are on the *sides* of their heads. Side Biters eat Hoop Worms mostly. It's kind of unfair though, because Hoop Worms can't see very well when they're rolling. If a Side Biter sees a Hoop Worm rolling in its direction, it sits down and pretends to be a big rock. If a Hoop Worm rolls too close to it, the Side Biter opens its mouth and, well, *eats it!* Isn't that terrible?"

"It eats *worms?* Totally gross!" Cathy said.

"Yes, isn't it?" said Doot. "Imagine, raw

34

worms. Unthinkable! But you know, when they're *baked* just right, they're actually quite..."

"Oh *yuck!*" cried Cathy and Danny.

"Well, I guess you'd just have to try one to know." Doot said.

Danny wanted to get his mind off of baked worms. He asked Doot, "What's the weirdest creature you've ever found?"

Doot thought for a moment and said, "The weirdest creature I've ever found? I'd have to say it was the Puff Bug. They're about as big as you are, except when they've been eating for a while.

"Puff Bugs eat a special kind of pink grass that grows on the planet where they live. The strange thing is, as they digest the grass in their stomachs they make a gigantic amount of stomach gas. They'll eat for weeks without a break. Eventually, they eat all the grass in one place, and they need to move on. By that time they've become so full of gas that they are puffed up dozens of times bigger than normal.

"Now here's the weird part. What happens to you when you eat too much and get a lot of gas trapped inside your stomach?"

"I burp!" said Cathy.

"Exactly," said Doot. "And that's just what the Puff Bug does. Except it does it in a most spectacular way. When a Puff Bug burps, it burps with so much gas and with such tremendous force that it blasts the creature right off the ground and into the next valley. If it's lucky, it has a nice safe flight and it lands in a place with lots of fresh pink grass."

"What if it isn't lucky?" Danny asked.

"Oh, then it's just the most awful thing you've ever seen!" exclaimed Doot. "Have you ever had the hiccups?"

Cathy and Danny nodded.

"If a Puff Bug hiccups while it's burping, which happens every now and then to older Puff Bugs, then the poor old Puff Bug... it, well, it just ... it just ..."

"It just what? What does it do?" Cathy demanded.

"It explodes!" said Doot. "Pieces of Puff Bug go flying everywhere, and that's the end of the poor creature. It's an incredible sight. Then the Puff Bug pieces fall back to the ground. They become a kind of fertilizer that helps the pink grass grow taller."

Doot created a floating picture of the scene for Cathy and Danny.

"That's just too weird," said Danny.

The bus came to the stop near their house. They all got off.

Doot sat on top of Danny's shoulders as they walked to Cathy and Danny's house. When they went inside, Cathy called out, "Mom! We're home! Is it okay if we have a friend stay for dinner tonight?"

They heard their mother call from another room. "That's fine. Get cleaned up and come on. Dinner's almost ready!"

DEFINITELY A NEW LOOK

Cathy, Danny and Doot walked into the bathroom. They saw themselves in the mirror above the sink.

"Doot," Cathy said. "I've been meaning to ask you. What do you really look like? All we can see are your clothes."

"I'll tell you what," Doot said. "You can play your guessing game with me. I'll tell you about the planet where I come from. You can guess what I look like. Start at the beginning. What do you know about me already?"

"You're small, and you come from a planet that's smaller than Earth," Cathy said. "Your planet hasn't got much gravity. That means you probably don't need much strength to move around. I'll bet you're pretty skinny."

"Yeah!" said Danny. "That explains why you were so easy to carry on my shoulders."

"Low gravity also means something else," Doot said. "I'll give you a clue. Think about gravity and the amount of air on the moon."

"If your planet has less gravity than Earth, then it also probably has less air," Cathy said. "I'll bet that means you've got to have really big lungs to be able to breathe in enough air to live."

"Not bad!" Doot said. "Here's how you might start to look if you lived a long time on my planet."

Doot made a strange whistling noise. Cathy and Danny were amazed at what they suddenly saw in the mirror. Their arms, legs, waists, and necks shrank and became very skinny. At the same time, their chests grew very large as their lungs grew bigger.

"That's awesome!" cried Danny.

"Oh, you're not done yet," Doot said. "Think about this. How are you supposed to fill those great big lungs through such puny noses?"

"You've got a really big nose, don't you!" Cathy laughed.

"Well, bigger than yours," said Doot. "And while you're at it, think about this. Sounds are harder to hear in thin air than in thick air."

"Then you need bigger ears to hear the sounds!" said Danny. "Big ears and a big nose! Wow! I'll bet you look funny!"

As soon as Danny said that, he and Cathy looked in the mirror and saw their ears and noses grow to giant sizes.

Danny stared at himself and asked a little nervously, "Um, this is only temporary, right?"

"It is unless you want me to make it permanent. I must say though, I think these changes make you look a lot better," Doot said.

"No no!" cried Danny. "Temporary is okay. We like the way we used to look just fine."

"Now then," Doot continued. "I'll tell you something else about my planet. We have a sun like you do. But we're farther from our sun that you are from yours. What do you suppose that might mean?"

"Well," Cathy began. "It's probably not as light on your planet in the daytime as it is here. That's probably why you're wearing sunglasses. I'll bet you've got bigger eyes than we do so you can see better in the dim light."

"Right!" said Doot. And with that, Cathy and Danny saw their eyes grow to the size of oranges.

"There's still one more thing you've left out," Doot said. "I'll give you another hint. If your planet were farther from your sun, how would you feel?"

40

"I'll bet we'd be a lot colder," Danny said. "I know! Your planet is probably colder than ours. You need some way to keep warm."

"Fur!" cried Cathy. As she said it, both she and Danny saw themselves become covered with thick, soft fur.

"Oh my gosh!" Cathy said. "This is *so* completely bizarre!"

"Now you look like me!" Doot said. In a twinkling, Doot removed the coat, sunglasses, boots, and hat.

The three skinny, furry creatures with enormous eyes, noses, ears, and lungs stared at each other. Then they began to howl with laughter.

Someone was pounding on the bathroom door. A voice boomed in at them from outside. "Dinner's on the table! What's going on in there? What's all that noise about? You'd better not be playing with the water or you'll be sorry!"

Danny yelled out, "No, it's okay Mom! We're just playing with Doot!"

"Doot?" their Mom yelled. "What kind of a name is that? Who is this new friend of yours anyway?"

"Doot? Well, Doot is... Doot is from out of town!" Danny yelled. He and Cathy began laughing again.

"Well, Doot-from-out-of-town," their mom said. "I think it's time we met. Don't you?"

Cathy and Danny looked at Doot, then at themselves in the bathroom mirror. They laughed and then yelled, "Sure Mom! Come on in!"

GLOSSARY

Atmosphere: A layer of gasses surrounding a planet. Earth's atmosphere is mostly nitrogen gas and oxygen gas.

Crater: A bowl-shaped hole left in the ground from a meteorite, asteroid, or some other object hitting the surface.

Erosion: The wearing down of surface features on a planet from water and wind.

Gravity: A property of all matter that causes it to attract and be attracted by all other matter.

Meteor: A glowing streak of light in the sky caused by a small piece of rock in outer space burning up in Earth's upper atmosphere. Also called a shooting star.

Meteorite: A piece of rock from space that falls through a planet's atmosphere and hits the ground.

Shooting star: Another name for a meteor.

46